Cat and Dog in a Mess

Written and illustrated by
Shoo Rayner

Slip! Slap! Slop!
Dog was in the mud.

Dog was a mess. Cat was not.

Dog let Cat pick the mud off.

A bit of mud was stuck on.

Cat had to cut the mud off.
Snip! Snip!

Dog got in the tub.
Rub-a-dub-dub!

Drip! Drip! Drip! Dog was wet.

Dog ran fast till he was not wet.

Dog was spick and span.

But Cat was in a mess!

Cat and Dog fell in the mud.

Dog is a mess and Cat is a mess.
Snap!

Cat

spick and span

Dog

in a mess

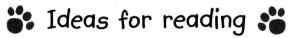 Ideas for reading

Written by Sue Graves cert. Ed (Distinction)
Primary Literacy Consultant

Learning objectives: Hear and say sounds in words in the order in which they occur; Extend vocabulary, exploring the meanings and sounds of new words; use their phonic knowledge to read simple regular words and make phonetically plausible attempts at more complex words.

Curriculum Links: Physical development: Recognise the importance of keeping healthy.

Focus phonemes: t (cat, tub, let, cut, not), ck (pick, stuck, spick), e (mess, let)

Other new phonemes: s, a, i, n, c, e, o, r, m, d, g, u, l, h, f, b

Fast words: was, the, to

Word count: 89

Getting started

- Write the words that feature the focus phonemes *t*, *ck* and *e* on a small whiteboard and ask the children to fast-read them, blending aloud if they need to.

- Look at the words *slip, slap, slop, stuck, snip, drip* and *fast* on the whiteboard. They all feature consonant clusters. Model how to blend the *s* and *l* together in *slip* and ask the children to try with the other words.

- Review the following irregular high frequency words: *the, was* and *to*. Select children to write these words on the whiteboard, from memory.

- Look at the front cover together. Ask the children to identify the two animals. *What are they are doing?*

Reading and responding

- Hand out the books to the children to read independently. Work round the children and listen in on them as they read. Check how they are coping with the words that feature the focus phonemes and consonant clusters.

- When the children have finished reading turn to p7 together. Ask them what *rub-a-dub-dub* means. *Why is it a good way to describe the dog washing himself?*

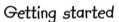